Kid-Sized

Dona Herweck Rice

Publishing Credits

Rachelle Cracchiolo, M.S.Ed., *Publisher*
Conni Medina, M.A.Ed., *Managing Editor*
Nika Fabienke, Ed.D., *Content Director*
Véronique Bos, *Creative Director*
Shaun N. Bernadou, *Art Director*
Carol Huey-Gatewood, M.A.Ed., *Editor*
Valerie Morales, *Associate Editor*
Courtney Roberson, *Senior Graphic Designer*

Image Credits: All images from iStock and/or
Shutterstock.

Teacher Created Materials
5301 Oceanus Drive
Huntington Beach, CA 92649-1030
www.tcmpub.com
ISBN 978-1-4938-9826-8

This is  .

small

That is  .
big

This is  .

small

That is  .

big

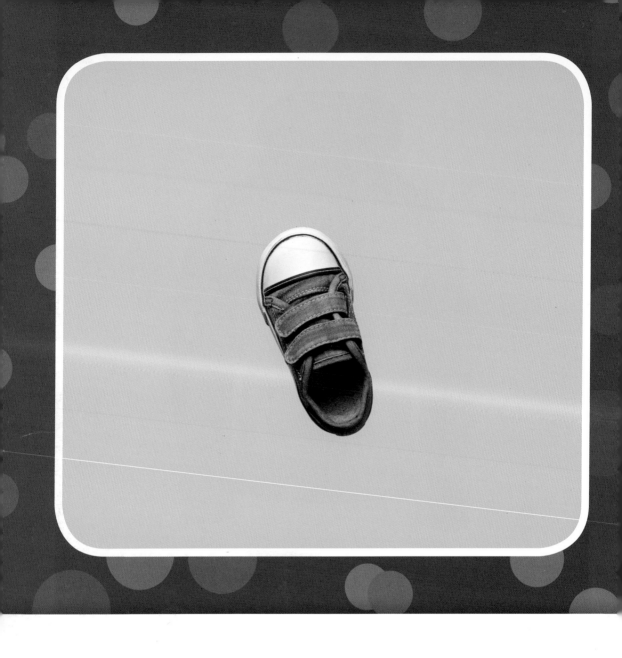

This is 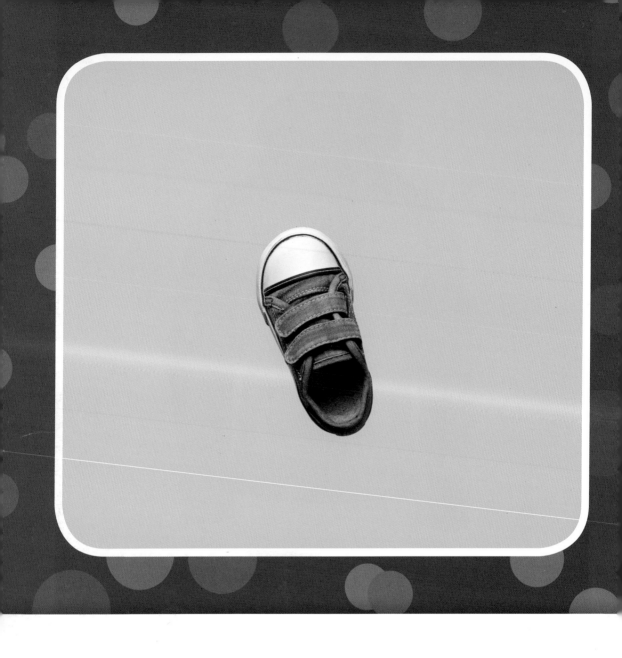 .

small

That is  .

big

This is  .

small

That is .

big

This is  .

small

That is  .

big

High-Frequency Words

is
that
this